To Senator Boxer—
Dare to dream!
Sue Pyatt
April 2004

Call Me
Madame President

To Everett, Jennifer, Laurie and Jeff whose encouragement made this book possible

First Edition

ISBN 0-9742575-0-8

Printed in the United States of America

IMAGINATION STATION PRESS
–a subsidiary of Snowspring Ltd.
Arlington, Virginia

Call Me
Madame President

By Sue Pyatt
Illustrated By Keith A. Gaston

When I have a piece of chalk,
I play hopscotch on my walk.

Sometimes I jump with all my might
and leap so far I'm out of sight.

If I land in a White House tree,
the Secret Service keep their eyes on me.

Want to know what it's like to be the President,
and a full-time White House resident?

Please come right in.
I'll tell you how it's been.

Yes, mmm-hmm, I know,
'cause it's me, Amanda.
I'm the leader of the show!

When I'm at home,
my brother Freddie likes to scoff,
"Eight isn't old enough.

You can't until you're thirty-five ya know.
Amanda, you have twenty-seven years to go."

I answer him, my voice quite low,
"Well, yes...and no."

8

'Cause in my IMAGINATION
as President, I'm a huge sensation.

This is me, the Chief,
in my Inaugural parade.

Get lost, Freddie boy.
This dream will never fade.

The Oval Office is my place
to tackle problems and set my pace.

My personal secretary Mr. Zook
keeps my appointments in a book.

11

There's always one more VIP
who wants to see me urgently.

We pack them in.
Then we begin:

schools, seniors, jobs, health care,
kids, farmers, crime, clean air.

Economics, war, and peace,
the action doesn't cease.

And I ask myself each day:
"What can I do to lead the way?"

13

Sometimes I travel across the sea
and my puppy, Coolidge, comes along with me.

For us, the most fun of all
is the day I throw the first baseball.

That's in the spring of every year.
Then the stadium crowd gives me a cheer.

15

I'm sure it won't surprise you sweeties that I attend a lot of meetings.

I meet with big shots who consent to help me run the government.

If I find I'm running late,
I can always roller-skate.

When fielding questions from the press,
I know how to show finesse.

I don't have time to skip a beat
and must think fast up on my feet.

Yes, I give some fancy parties
for diplomats and other smarties.

State dinners remind me of a magic fable
when kings and queens dine at my table.

My puppy, Coolidge, likes state dinners too.
If he doesn't chew on someone's shoe,

we let him stay and gawk
until he needs his evening walk.

As Commander-in-Chief, I'm a symbol of success.
To meet the troops, I designed my patriotic dress.

When it comes to speaking, I don't balk.
Mom always says I love to talk.

21

My State of the Union Address is on TV.
I make it before Congress and the world community.

CANDY

RESERVED 1ST DOG

PIZZA BOX
PHONE BOOK
STATE LAWS
SHOPPERS GUIDE
WORLD ATLAS

I tell Congress in the best part of my dream:
"All the kids and animals are on my special team.

To the ones in need, my team and I give aid
so that none are hungry or afraid."

I conclude, "I am not hesitant
to use my power as President."

During this amazing TV speech,
my startled family starts to screech.

Dad shouts to Mom,
"Our daughter has great leadership ability
which clearly comes from you and me!"

At the end of every busy day
I want to yell, "Olé."

'Cause I've done my very best
and certainly deserve a rest.

27

I love the next part of my dream:
Freddie opens my White House bedroom door
and says, "I'm sorry I was mean before.

Since you're President at this early date,
how about me for Secretary of State?"

I give Freddie a little smile
and reply, "I'll think about it for a while."

So in the Lincoln bed I finally fall
and say, "Good night, God bless to one and all."

THE END

Index of Pictured Places in Washington, D.C.